GRIM TALES

SOUTHERN ADVENTURES

Edited by Sarah Washer

First published in Great Britain in 2015 by:

 Young**Writers**

Remus House
Coltsfoot Drive
Peterborough
PE2 9BF
Telephone: 01733 890066
Website: www.youngwriters.co.uk

Printed and bound in the UK by BookPrintingUK
Website: www.bookprintinguk.com

FOREWORD

Welcome, Reader!

For Young Writers' latest competition, Grim Tales, we gave secondary school pupils nationwide the tricky task of writing a story with a beginning, middle and an end in just 100 words. They could either write a completely original tale or add a twist to a well-loved classic. They rose to the challenge magnificently!

We chose stories for publication based on style, expression, imagination and technical skill. The result is this entertaining collection full of diverse and imaginative mini sagas, which is also a delightful keepsake to look back on in years to come.

Here at Young Writers our aim is to encourage creativity in young adults and to inspire a love of the written word, so it's great to get such an amazing response, with some absolutely fantastic stories. This made it a tough challenge to pick the winners, so well done to Jasmine Barron who has been chosen as the best author in this anthology.

I'd like to congratulate all the young authors in Grim Tales - Southern Adventures - I hope this inspires them to continue with their creative writing. And who knows, maybe we'll be seeing their names on the best seller lists in the future...

Jenni Bannister

Editorial Manager

CONTENTS

Trinity School, Teignmouth

Wilson's School, Wallington

THE MINI SAGAS

THE HOODED VENGEANCE

I gazed across the skyline at the great giants of the New York City skyline. The wind brushed like a feather over my hands, which were worn by hardened warfare and brutal experience. It had to be done. I had a mission. But was it worth it? I hoped so. As I sauntered to the searing drop on the edge of the skyscraper I recollected the memories of my severe and deadly mistakes. I picked it up. It felt heavy but was cold just like my heart. My surroundings slowed. My heart pounded. *Thump. Thump. Thump.* And I committed murder.

HARRY REGAN (13)

CHANGING FACES

She ran from the little cottage. She'd alienated her whole family. No, they weren't her family, they were beasts; ferocious bears. Her family were gone, all except for sweet, naive Gran. She knew where she had to go. She heard a roaring scream behind her. She quickened her pace. Not long until she reached Grandma's. A golden curl fell in her face. That would have to go if she wanted to remain undetected. She may even get a hood to hide behind. Blood-red. That sounded good. A new identity and a new life. No longer Goldie, but Little Red.

HEATHER LOUISE CALVER (16)

ARTHUR

Arthur pulled back the string and aimed at the apple, *Twang*. Yet his arrow only grazed it and Kay's split the apple in half. *Why is it that Kay always won*? he thought.

The next day they would be fighting with real swords. Before the contest Arthur felt Kay's sword, it was light but his was heavy. 'Now everyone would think that Kay should be king.'

Sure enough before long, Arthur was lying on the ground weaponless. Suddenly, he spotted a sword embedded in a rock. Though all others failed, he pulled it out, so becoming King Arthur!

JOSEPH WITCHALLS (11)

LITTLE RED

'Little Red, Little Red!' her mother called. She dragged her legs, took the basket, continued to stall, for this journey was long, filled with wolves and all. And the smell of the brownies made her stomach bawl.
Through trees to Grandma's house, she went, the smell, lingering, causing torment. She became restless, a feeling of Lent, breaking her mother's trust, she ate, worst intent.
Now as she sat and nibbled, mind on food, she failed to realise the wolf, and his plans to intrude. *But, this is too easy*, he said in his head. So went; ate her grandmother instead.

LAUREN RACHEL DINNALL (14)

MISUNDERSTOOD

The witch stared at the ground, glumly. Nobody seemed to want to be friends with her. It wasn't the witch's fault that her cat had accidently spilt poison on the apple that she'd given to Snow White. Or that the dodgy tradesman had sold her a spinning wheel with a sleeping draught in the needle. And she was merely babysitting Rapunzel but her parents never turned up again! But nobody ever let the witch explain herself for the stories had been passed around so much that they were nothing like the events that actually took place.

MAYA SANKARAN (13)

GLOVES

The snow was bitterly cold. We were outside making snowmen. My phone rang so I took off my gloves and answered my phone. They fell to the ground. The phone call ended and I forgot about my gloves as I headed home.

I was watching TV, someone knocked at the door - outside stood a hooded figure. 'Are these yours?' he said as he handed me the gloves.

I replied, 'Yes, how did you know that they were mine?' I looked up but he was gone. The mysterious figure will forever be remembered.

MEGAN BARWICK (13)

DO YOU WANT TO FLY TO NEVERLAND?

There was someone else in the room. A boy. It was queer, she mused, how upon sunrise each morning he'd turn to air, despite his return the following night. It was difficult to see through the gloom, but in her mind's eye she knew him down to the most intricate detail. She smiled at her watcher, and for once, he responded. 'Do you want to fly to Neverland, Wendy?' She nodded and he led her towards the open window, sprinkling stardust upon her head. But there's no such thing as magic, nor such a person as Peter Pan. They jumped.

REBECCA JEFFERY

I Flew On

Here, short days ago, my horse's hooves were thundering as I urged him onwards in a useless attempt to be home before dark. The little light of the setting sun which could filter through the dense foliage cast the thicket in a golden glow. Shouts and snarls came closer, as the edge of a cliff forced me to halt. Soon, I was thrown at a man's feet. Our eyes met, both brimming with hatred. As his repulsive arms reached forwards, I lashed out. My captors finished, I galloped again. Only this time, when I reached the cliff, I flew on.

Sabah Athar (14)

IN SEARCH FOR ANOTHER...

The clock strikes 12 as the moon shines brightly like a diamond. I am hungry for my next victim. This time I want an intelligent, beautiful and old one. The streets are misty and they're beginning to close in on me. I notice her juicy, red apples for eyes that glisten. I smile in excitement; for the apples or for my target? Obviously, I know what I'm attracted to. She doesn't turn around so I do what I'm best at. RIP! In the same way as I did yesterday and the day before. Yes that's me... Jack the Ripper!

TAYIBHA JAHAN (13)

THE HANDSOME PRINCE

I held onto my glass slipper tightly and waited for her to reappear in the mist. The clock struck twelve again and I stared at the brightly lit moon which stood beautifully. When I turned around, she was there; walking elegantly towards me. Like a hungry wolf who had just found his prey, I knelt down and placed the slipper on her delicate foot. It was smooth. It fitted perfectly. It was her! I looked up and felt my blood boil viciously as my hand moved towards her glistening throat. I was ready for her. Cinderella was finally mine!

RAZEEN ABDUL

CHARLIE AND THE CHOKE-LET FACTORY

My wildest dream had finally come true. I could just imagine all the delicious, scrumptious, tooth-rotting sweets lined up against the liquorice walls. Strawberry spirals and blueberry bonbons! All the sweets to my heart's desire. Well, actually my stomach's. The audience glared at me with green-eyed envy as I waltzed up to the factory. I opened the elaborate doors and jerked to a sudden halt. Choke collars lined the sterile walls. Bodies lay strewn across the floor. Decapitated. A deranged looking man, with vibrantly orange coloured hair, stared at me. His mouth stretched into a wide grimace. 'You're next.'

PRASHINA HARJANI (14)
Ark Academy, Wembley

Violet Aurora

Pain. Darkness. Eyes tightly shut. He struggled to recalculate his balance, he had to shuffle his way around, that was a high enough calibre. This new inception of events has also left him increasingly stressed. His mental state imploded in a supernova of thought and emotion - elation, fear, melancholy, fury, queasiness and most importantly, insanity. A war of his sanity battled under his skin and bones in his mind. A flare of purple. Vibrant colours, granting his imaginary sight. He dawdled aimlessly in this sea of darkness, slowly succumbing to the only solution that was exclusively available now. Madness

Damian Alvarez (14)
Ark Academy, Wembley

The Unfortunate Case
Of Hansel And Gretel

A tale of death, deception and desertion. Out in the woods anything goes. An unsuspecting father left behind his vulnerable children. An evil witch arose from the deep depths to grab her opportunity to strike. She made Hansel eat, eat, eat. She made Gretel clean, clean, clean. Now she's in the oven baking away. Evil stepmother gone, she could not possibly stay! Hansel was beheaded by the witch's son! Gretel's life ended by a bullet from his gun! The unsuspecting father left all alone, his sorrow can still be heard, his cry, his grief, his groan!

Kai Franklin (14)
Ark Academy, Wembley

BEYOND DEATH

Death, arrived to Megara, Hercules' true love. Hope was lost within the wilderness. That she wouldn't ever awaken, never shine her smile to the world again. However, that wasn't the end. Hercules, drenched from tears, gasped as he saw her body inflate and deflate once more. Although her eyes were shut, her charm was radiant against his face. Skin as smooth as silk. Her red hair flowing impeccably on her shoulder blades. Megara laid peacefully until her eyes flickered open, revealing bloodshot, red eyes. She growled. That's when she munched on her past lover, spurting blood all over the place.

NADINE ALOSERT
Ark Academy, Wembley

Broken Mirror

Her ebony hair danced through the room. She stopped. Her scarlet lips spoke the words, 'Mirror, mirror on the wall, who's the fairest of them all?'
A shimmering face extruded from the mirror. 'The one that follows you.' Liquid metal seeped through the creaky, wooden door. It engulfed the pale skin, leaving an aged woman, with charcoal lips. She tried to scream, but her lips were entangled in suffering and hate. The mirror showed a vibrant, young woman, with sapphire eyes. 'I am the fairest of them all.' Her voice echoed the room, filling it with envy and revenge.

Klio Balliu (14)
Ark Academy, Wembley

STRANGE DREAM OF UNWANTED LOVE

She shuffled through the deteriorated skeletons. Her eyes shocked with intimidation. There were 30, 40, or even more piles of them. Her surroundings started spinning, making her view blurry. The pulverised skeletons reciprocated into humans. No, ghosts. Their eyes reflected sadness, neither revenge nor anger. 'I wanted nothing but the love of my child.'
'I love my child more than anything.' Everyone spoke of something they wanted to tell someone. Their words made her eyes fill with tears; she closed her eyes with consternation. When she opened her eyes again everything seemed impalpable except the tears in her eyes.

ANUGRAHA DAS (13)
Ark Academy, Wembley

A Twisted Fate: The Beast Within

The music ended. He took her hand and led her out onto the balcony. They sat on the marbled bench, gazing affectionately into each other's eyes. Beside them sat the enchanted rose encased in a glassed confinement. Only one last petal remained. Finally, the Beast thought, *oh, how many years he'd waited for it to wilt.*
'It's so beautiful,' she spoke.
'Its beauty does not compare to yours.' He forced as little hatred as he could into every syllable.
He willed the petal to fall, but not before he leaned in and sank his teeth into her flesh. Petal falls.

Sara Arybou (14)
Ark Academy, Wembley

LOOKING GLASS

There on the wall it stayed, see-though as always. It holds lives and souls. She dashed cautiously towards the glass. She tried to grab it. The monsters appeared from behind, as she screamed for help the monster grew angry with despair to keep her quiet. They snapped her neck in a swift movement. Then silence. Footsteps could be heard for miles. The monster hid in the shadows, as the young group approached. The group had no idea who had screamed but they saw the glass ball and approached but failed to make it. There was silence, silence that killed.

LEANNE MARIE ROBINSON-HILLS (14)
Ark Academy, Wembley

THE FOLLOWERS

The melodious tune of his manipulative flute infected the village as the innocent children were submissive to his music. The synchronised footsteps behind him created a sinister smile to creep across his face. 'Follow me children,' he said enticingly. His crooked fingers lured the children towards him.

However, the children began to smirk with mischief, their heads simultaneously tilting sideways as they slowly revealed sharp daggers, 'You can't fool us,' they chanted. Quivering in fear, the petrified piper turned, slamming his back against a wall as a dagger struck through his heart like lightning. 'Dig in friends. Dinner is served.'

VEESHA GAJJAR (14)
Ark Academy, Wembley

THE ROOTS OF POCAHONTAS

'Grandmother Willow!' Pocahontas slyly smirked, her charcoal hair draped across her figure. Opaque eyes sunk into her soul, an axe entangled between her fingertips, hidden behind thighs, concealed by her glowing skin, glowing smile, growing lies.
'Pocahontas darling!' the implacable tree replied. The willow's weak leaves gestured to embrace Pocahontas for an unexpected hug. Pocahontas no longer smug. Withdrew the axe with force in hand, no longer a smile, no longer a tan. A corpse lies dead in Grandmother Willow's soil bed. Pocahontas laid helpless, an axe through her stomach, she was fed. Grandmother Willow's secrets all shown not said.

ANNIE MARK (13)
Ark Academy, Wembley

FINAL DESTINATION

I ran and ran with the thing chasing me. I woke up with beads of sweat rolling down my face. A *bang* at my door. I was scared. I thundered down the stairs, flung open the door. There were two men in black suits. One said it was time. I already knew what they were talking about. After the longest car trip, they took me to a room with a door at the end and left. I had many questions, why me? I'm too young to die. Can't they find another way? I opened the door and walked into darkness.

ALEXANDER TOWN-PHILLS (13)
Ark Academy, Wembley

THE SEEKER

It was my fault. My contaminated womb revealed the light to the unwelcome soul. Disloyalty stung my veins as he now took his faint and last breath. His miniature crystal eyes locked. His lips tightened into the perfect heart. *Bang!* The fool no longer belonged. My eyes penetrated his. He paced towards the soul, his eyes glazed as if he had chosen his next victim. My heart sank. His disfigured claws removed the soul's heart. The heart hung on my own. I froze. With that came the death of the only humanity left and with the birth of the seeker.

MARINA NAVES (13)
Ark Academy, Wembley

INTO THE UNKNOWN

There he stood. Lost. In the unknown woods by himself in the dark. He turned around and saw a mysterious looking building. The windows looked like eyes staring through to the back of his soul. Cautiously he entered the house. He found a torch and turned it on. As soon as he turned it on bats came flapping past him. Out of shock he fell to the cockroach infested floor. He immediately got back up. He saw a light switch and turned it on. There was a knock on the door. He opened it and saw a shadowy figure.

MAKAI PAYNE (14)
Ark Academy, Wembley

PATHWAY

He was being chased. His heart was beating at a unstoppable pace. Sweat began pouring down his face. The only thought he had was of what his mum would say. His foot buckled on bark that was on the floor. He blacked out. He woke up in an unknown house, looking at the Empire State Building. He began to panic. Then he heard a beeping sound. *Beep. Beep. Beep.* Then he saw a tag on his leg counting down. It was on zero. *Bang*! His body floated in the air, landing in all kinds of pieces on the floor.

TYREKE ROBINSON (14)
Ark Academy, Wembley

UNTITLED

Rapunzel looked down the tower as the prince climbed up her hair. He was tugging at her head a bit and she didn't like it so she decided to cut it. He fell down and just lay there still. She didn't know what to do so she jumped down to see if he was OK but it turned out he was dead. She'd killed him. She closed his eyes, then picked up his body (it was very heavy) and chucked it into the lake around the tower hoping that nobody would see it. She couldn't believe she had done it.

SAMANTHA WATT (12)
Barnfield Vale Academy, Dunstable

FROSTY SNOW VENTURE

Some time had passed since the seven dwarfs helped Snow White. At this moment, they'd already left to find a new meaning in life. Unfortunately, it was winter and the snow had fully taken over. Snow cascaded upon them as they effortlessly trudged through. Meanwhile, Dopey stumbled across a mound in the snow... Dopey alerted the others and all scrounged through. After a few seconds, they found out it was. No... Snow White! Scraping it away, it only confirmed their suspicions. Terrified of what would happen next and grieving, they took her body and gave her a proper burial.

RHYDIAN CHIKU (12)
Barnfield Vale Academy, Dunstable

LEMON SLICES

She waltzed around the freshly-made bed, taking in the familiar
scent, gently caressing her kitten. Her mum knew she wouldn't be
long. Screaming brought her back. She danced along the edge of
the well, teasing it when she stumbled over a minute rock, collapsing
into the well. She awoke on the other side, strange creatures looming
over her. They held up something, putting it to their eyes. 'It's your
turn... The Darkness wants you…' It was gleaming in the neon light,
the seeds standing out in the yellow membrane. She was dragged
upwards, into a light, then - gone…

MORGAN VANHOEKE (13)
Barnfield Vale Academy, Dunstable

THE WALK

The sun was starting to set and the wind was whistling. Sonia was tired and wanted to go home. James insisted that they walk for longer. He wanted the right place. Sonia caught a glimpse of a dark figure lurking in the background. Something was wrong, she could feel it in the air. James heard Sonia gasping for air, there she was, dead on the floor. 'No Sonia! Why?' He took the ring out of his pocket and placed it on her finger. Gently giving her one last kiss on the forehead. He turned away with sorrow and walked away.

LAUREN HART (13)
Barnfield Vale Academy, Dunstable

ONCE A VICTIM, ALWAYS A VICTIM...

Snow White had missed the seven dwarfs; she could barely stop herself from squealing with eagerness. She strolled up the path, leading to the magnificent mansion, and walked in. Spacious. Sophisticated. She already knew she would love it.
On her first night, she was drifting away into a beautiful sleep... then, there was a noise. She delicately tiptoed down the spiral staircase, to find a note. When she moved here, she thought that her blackmailer wouldn't be able to find her, she was wrong, they did find her, along with the paramedics. Draped in a pool of blood...

JASMYN GIBSON (12)
Barnfield Vale Academy, Dunstable

TRAPPED!

There I was standing with Ted in a lightless, abandoned warehouse. We shouldn't be here. We look around until we can see and stare at a luminous green splodge on the wall. Ted goes to carelessly touch the blob when all of a sudden, the green bogey-like spot fell off the wall, and started increasing in size quickly until it was humanlike. The blob started running towards us, screaming, 'You will die.' There we were trapped in a warehouse, with no doors or windows, we were just waiting in the corner for a miracle. We are crying for help.

HARRY CHAPMAN (13)
Barnfield Vale Academy, Dunstable

MELINA'S ETERNAL WISH

Melina, granddaughter of King Arthur's advisor, the wizard Merlin, was running through a desolate land. Running from King Arthur, not getting far before he kept catching up to her, slashing at her back, blood dripping. With her death near, Arthur told her he was immortal, she fought back with magic; striking him down and taking his immortality, to create her own eternal world, where nothing ever died. Not humans, not animals, not anything. And so, only one thing stood in her way: A knight, swift as the wind, wielding Caliburn, Excalibur's sheath, and Excalibur the sword. Death was inevitable.

GEORGE ALDRIDGE (13)
Barnfield Vale Academy, Dunstable

Jen And The Demon Shape Shifter

Jen was eight when her mother perished, three years passed and still all she thought about was her mum.

One day she was taking a nonchalant promenade in the village, when antithesis the street she saw a figure which looked exactly like her mother; it was, but only she was different. Jen ran across the street and said, 'Mum, is that you?'

'Yes,' replied the figure.

'I've missed you.'

Suddenly the figure transformed... into an evil creature with demonic purposes, also piercing red eyes. She grabbed Jen from the village, flew into the air, never to be seen again.

Sydnie McKechnie (13)
Barnfield Vale Academy, Dunstable

THE BOY AND THE KILLER SNAKE

In the forest a young boy, Jamie, was walking around wearily searching for his house. Jamie was lost for more than a week and was dying for food and drink. Suddenly, out of nowhere, a killer snake appeared right next to him. That really gave him a shock. Like a girl being scared of a spider but instead it was a boy and a snake. Jamie had a fear of forest creatures so he tried to run as fast as he could, but the snake was just teasing him and grabbed poor Jamie and ate him messily.

CHE KABALAN (12)
Barnfield Vale Academy, Dunstable

THE CRUEL MOON

The full moon crept out from behind the clouds. I started changing; fur grew all over my skin getting thicker and thicker like a fur coat. My feet stretched until they ripped the leather of my shoes. My toenails on both feet became thin, pointed and curled. Fangs protruded from my mouth. Everything became clearer; I could hear things from a further distance. All my senses had been enhanced. Kyle looked at me, shocked; 'Jason, what's happening to you?' I couldn't control myself; next thing I knew there was a puddle of blood on the floor. I'd killed Kyle.

BRADEN KEEBLE (13)
Barnfield Vale Academy, Dunstable

THE VAMPIRES AND HER

The girl entered the house. She walked into the living room to find the room in darkness. She took a step into the room when she saw something peculiar. She saw blood, human blood! She turned and walked into the bathroom, through the darkness she heard water running, the tap had been left running and the water was spilling out. Walking into the kitchen she found her mother lying there, dead with two blood marks on her neck, around the kitchen table stood three vampires slowly falling to the floor at the sight of daylight. The girl stood. Motionless.

ASHLEIGH CLARIDGE (12)
Barnfield Vale Academy, Dunstable

THE TRIPLETS AND THE HOUSE

The triplets lived in a cottage with their mother and stepfather. The mum and stepfather were poor and were planning to get rid of them. The family had visions of dying from starvation.

Late that night they all went for a stroll into the woods and all of a sudden the triplets were lost, scared and isolated in the gloomiest midnight of the year. The triplets came across a strange house made of candy. They ate it and died, as it was poisonous. The owner of the house was a witch. When she saw the dead triplets she cackled wickedly.

ANASTASIA CHRISTOFI (13)
Barnfield Vale Academy, Dunstable

GOLDILOCKS ADVENTURE

Goldilocks stood silently, biting her lip. Her bloodshot eyes were looking around, she was hungry and tired. Golilocks walked on not knowing where she was going. Suddenly, she came upon a dark, small cottage, it looked deserted but she carried on walking to the cottage. She opened the door and walked in, luckily there was a light. The stairs groaned as she walked on them and in the corner of the house was a figure, it was grinning at her. She made a blood-curdling scream and ran out. The creature shouted, 'You should always knock before you enter.'

AIMEE HYDE (12)
Barnfield Vale Academy, Dunstable

UNTITLED

The old woman squirmed, trying to free herself from Red's ropes but she remained tied to the chair, gagged, watching them shove fistfuls of her money into a small woven basket. Part of Red felt guilty, but this woman wasn't exactly a saint either, yet she didn't deserve what happened next. It was so quick, just a blur of blood and screaming. Red tried to help her, being not totally immoral; but then those demonic eyes turned to her.

Seconds later, the wolf's head was on the floor, the woodsman towering behind its crumpled body.

That is the real story.

OLIE BURTON (13)
Broadlands Academy, Bristol

THE SECRET OF RAPUNZEL

In a lonely tower lived a girl named Rapunzel. She had a secret no one knew. On the day the prince began to climb to save her from a wicked witch something terrible happened, as he climbed he fell right back down along with all of Rapunzel's hair! She stood at the top, her pale round head shone as white as the moon. Rapunzel was in shock. The handsome prince discovered her secret. Her beautiful, blonde hair had always been a wig! The wicked witch was not a witch after all, but just her ashamed mother.

KATIE PAGE (13)
Broadlands Academy, Bristol

UNTITLED

Once upon a time there was a boy who was the son of a king. He was a nice boy who lived with his parents. He was happy. Suddenly, everything went wrong. His parents died in the war. He had to live with an evil fairy who was disguised as an old woman, she cursed him to live as a beast. He was forced to live alone in his parents' old castle, waiting for his true love to break the curse.

Years later, it all changed when a mysterious, old woman came to his castle, changing his life forever.

AMIR RADWAN (12)
Broadlands Academy, Bristol

THE LEGEND OF THE RED WATERFALLS

Cayfutray, a beautiful tribal girl, lived with her evil aunt in the forests of Native America. Before dying, her mother gave Cayfutray an exceptional power, 'You can transform into a body of water to save someone's life.'

She fell in love with a kind, young man, John from England. When they spent time together, angry aunt insinuated that their association would bring bad luck to the village. To escape the mob's fury, Cayfutray morphed herself into a waterfall and John turned into a rock. Witnessing this Aunt went mad. Folklore suggests whenever evil Aunt asks for forgiveness, waterfall turns red.

MANSHA SAHAY (13)
Burnham Grammar School, Slough

THE PSYCHO

Frantically bouncing around, screaming at the top of her voice, she destroyed everything in her way. Finally, she came to a stop, in front of a huge wooden door. Smashing her way through, she came across a sweet family of bears. Growling and moaning she punched her way through their cottage. She tilted her head, gave them a sick smile and grabbed their neck and shook them until they burst and couldn't breathe. Her brother made his way to the cottage and found three dead bears laying on the floor. He grabbed her stiff arm and dragged her away.

MIYA BETHANY BROWN (12)
Burnt Mill Academy, Harlow

CHASE

I sprinted down a narrow, gloomy alleyway but I didn't know why. So I stopped. Obtaining my breath, I ached.

'Stop!' yelled two policemen. My legs seemed to carry me into an abandoned, disintegrated house. I could feel soggy, scrunched up paper underneath me. Silhouettes darted down the alley, missing me completely. Thoughts; *why were those men chasing me*? *How did I get here*?

Unexpectedly, I began being hunted again. However, not by the police but by dogs. Giant, hungry dogs! I dashed. I fell. They bit.

I woke surrounded in sweat. It was a dream.

LOIS GOODGE
Burnt Mill Academy, Harlow

GOLDILOCKS AND THE THREE BEARS

We arrived home to find something strange and unsettling had happened to our house. My porridge bowl was empty, my chair was broken and the house felt weird. I was so upset that my chair had been destroyed, that I ran upstairs.

Laying in my bed, fast asleep, was a young girl. What was she doing there? As I called for Daddy Bear, she woke up, looking petrified. Daddy came upstairs, looking furious. I didn't know what he would do, so I ran out of the room. I heard screaming, crying and then silence.

ANNABEL RIVOIRE (12)
Burnt Mill Academy, Harlow

LITTLE RED RIDING HOOD

Once upon a time there lived a girl called Little Red. One day, her mother said, 'Red go see Gran, she's sick!' So off Little Red went into the deep, dark forest to get to Gran's.
All of a sudden she bumped into a wolf who said, 'You shouldn't be out here on your own,' She didn't care, she just walked up to the door. 'Little Red my dear, come in, your mother told me you were coming!' She went in and the last her gran saw was Little Red and a knife.

ROSE GAYNOR-BIZZELL
Burnt Mill Academy, Harlow

THE THREE LITTLE CANNIBALS

Oink! Oink! The three ravenous pigs chased after the wolf wanting to quench their thirst on his blood. They wanted to feast on his flesh and rip him apart, limb by limb. However, the wolf came prepared, he had built a house made of bricks. 'You'll never take me alive!' bellowed the wolf. The vicious pigs ripped off bricks with their bare hands. They decided to cook him in his own blood for extra flavour. They were sure that Jamie Oliver would approve of their tongue tingling dish. They left the best till last, the eyes.

TOM GROVE
Burnt Mill Academy, Harlow

THE PIGS' FINEST HOUSE

Long ago, there was a big, bad wolf with black fur and deadly fangs. He hadn't eaten for days on end and needed a meal. Meanwhile two pink pigs were in their brother's brick mansion enjoying the latest episode of Pigglebox. Suddenly they saw the lurking silhouette of the wolf outside the window. They boarded up the doors and windows and finally they placed giant metal spikes in the fireplace in case he came down the chimney. Sure enough, he did and landed straight on the spikes. The pigs then enjoyed themselves a midnight feast and new coats.

GEORGE W PITTMAN (13)
Burnt Mill Academy, Harlow

THE TWENTY PIGS

There were twenty, now there is three. When they were younger, twenty of them got put out in an iron cage and left to starve. After a week, they were so skinny they were all getting bad ideas and then they all started to try and eat each other. No pig stopped. They all ate the weakest first, after fifteen minutes there were sixteen dead pigs and the three little fat pigs all ganged up on the one pig left on its own. That was it, it was just the three pigs left. They are now coming for the farmer!

JENSON REDLER (13)
Burnt Mill Academy, Harlow

SNOW WHITE AND THE SEVEN SLAUGHTERS

She is smiling demonically as she is walking into our house. I don't know who she is but she seems like a psychopath. She stalks around the house before pulling the enormous knife out from the kitchen. She puts on an innocent looking face but I don't believe her. She raises the knife as my six brothers come through the door and freeze as they see the satanic girl in the middle of our small house. Slowly, she creeps towards us, we all look horrified. She pulls up the knife and slice, chop. Dead...

CHLOE HARRIS
Burnt Mill Academy, Harlow

DRAGON'S WORLD

There once was a dragon, Miles. He battled evil dragons who try to take his land.
One day he battled a dragon named Drew, this dragon was even harder than he expected, therefore he was defeated. It was a sad time for Miles because he could no longer stay where he had lived for some many years, he now had to live on his own.
Later, after searching for a place to live, Miles found a nice cave, but it was nowhere near as good as his old place. Well I guess that's dragons for you.

KIERAN ANDREW ROBERTSON (12)
Burnt Mill Academy, Harlow

THE MYSTERY OF TRINTON BAY

Tanya looked across the soothing ocean that surrounded her, she was alone on the island 'Trinton Bay', where she'd been abandoned. This was all because of her twin, Deborah, who asked her to race her to the rock just off the coast of Emerald, where Tanya used to live. She raced to the centre, through the trees of the forest. Then she came across an abandoned ship, also on the mysterious island, it looked like it had been there for ages, she crept inside. Then, she came face-to-face with the most feared monster in all of humanity, a ghost... *gulp*.

GEORGIA SAMUELS (12)
Burnt Mill Academy, Harlow

THE AXE WOLF

The Axe Wolf is a hideous wolf monster that comes out every night killing humans with his two axes. The Axe Wolf normally kills his victims by putting an axe in their back and then eats them with blood goring out of his mouth. He first rips off their limps and uses them as chopsticks, then he eats their body. He eats their head last so they can have their last dying breath as they are still alive. The Axe Wolf has murdered more than two thousand people. The Axe Wolf is a monstrous beast never seen to man.

RYAN BANHAM
Burnt Mill Academy, Harlow

ONE LAST BREATH

As he walked up the creaking stairs he could sense something was out of place. He felt an unearthly presence. He turned around, lost his footing and stumbled to the ground. As he picked himself up something kicked him to the ground. He looked up and saw a shadowy figure looming over him. He lashes out at him but it was no one. His hands were just slipping through its body like it was a ghost. Then the ghost cackles and poses his body. The man can't stop himself walking towards a window, then screams.

JACOB FINN
Burnt Mill Academy, Harlow

HANSEL AND GRETEL

Once upon a time Hansel and Gretel got dumped in the forest by their evil stepmother. All they were given was a slice of bread each. They ripped up the bread and placed down the crumbs so they could retrace their steps. The crumbs were eaten by the animals in the forest. Hansel and Gretel got lost; they found a cottage made of candy. The witch inside asked them to come in, so they did. The witch trapped them both in cages. Once they were fat enough she cooked them and ate them for dinner.

LUKE DAVID WHEATLAND (11)
Burnt Mill Academy, Harlow

BERT THE BANANA

At 11 Kawaii Lane, some strange happenings have occurred involving a toaster and a slice of bread. Some witnesses have said they saw the bread coming out of the toaster unbelievably tanned. The Secret Kitchen Services had come to a conclusion. They had to call out their top spy, Bert the Banana. He swings, he jumps and he crawls, just to get the right viewing point of the suspect. Because Bert is such a good spy, he caught them straight away. The bread was being eaten by the humans! What a waste of such tanned bread! Poor Bert.

APRIL ROSE FIFIELD (12)
Burnt Mill Academy, Harlow

THE FROG PRINCE

The princess was so chuffed. She had just been asked for her hand by the man of her dreams! What more could she ask for? He was a handsome, young man, with flowing blond hair, cut in the latest style, of course, handsome blue eyes, a pure, bleachy smile, not to mention the fact that he knew all of the latest trends.

She expressed her extreme happiness by locking him in a sticky kiss that slowly became stickier, and stickier, and a long tongue began probing her mouth.

'Ribbit!'

'Aiiiiieeeeeeeee!' she screamed, casting the disgusting amphibian down to the floor.

MARCUS STANSBURY (12)
Chiltern Hills Academy, Chesham

THE PINK SKY

The sky permanently pink in hue; animals were bejewelled. One white dove outshone the rest with a star upon her head. It was placed by Cinderella, a reward for helping every night of the ball.
The dove visited Cinderella. Her castle was hidden behind an array of emerald trees, owls perched along the branches. Cinderella was on her bed sobbing.
The king hadn't returned from battle, Cinderella was due to bear a child. The dove flew off to tell the king of Cinderella's news. He rushed home and was just in time, the baby was named Star after the bird.

CHLOE ELLEN ALHADEFF (11)
Chiltern Hills Academy, Chesham

THE VINE

There was a flash of gold. He climbed up this gold vine, hoping it would be strong enough to hold his weight. He climbed over the window sill and onto the cold cobblestone floor. She turned around, which brought horror to the young prince's face, he didn't think she would look like this. He looked at her hand and saw the red stains over her ugly fingers and his eyes went straight to the silver weapon in her hand. She walked over several corpses and pointed the blade right into his heart. An agonising screech filled the tower.

ADEL ZAKRZEWSKI (11)
Chiltern Hills Academy, Chesham

CINDERELLA AND THE BLOOD RED APPLE

'Yes Cinderella,' mumble the sisters simultaneously as they reluctantly polish a glass slipper.

'Stepmother! My fairy godmother will be here in a minute with prince Charming! I cannot attend the ball wearing a dress with no sequins,' whines Cinderella dramatically, combing her long, silky locks.

Minutes later, Cinderella is in a graceful carriage with her prince, unsuspectingly munching on a blood-red apple. She looks up, concerned, 'This isn't the way to the... ' but she didn't finish her sentence. Victory for the godmother and prince. Cinders, poisoned, is abandoned in the dark, eerie forest. But is she alone?

IMOGEN FARMERY (11)
Chiltern Hills Academy, Chesham

HANSEL AND GRETEL

The witch laughed an evil laugh to herself. In the middle of the deep, dark forest, some helpless crumbs of bread were scattered along the path. The witch instantly thought of children and planned a grand feast. She followed the trail to find a young boy and a young girl. She immediately thought to lure them back to her fortress. The children slowly turned around. The witch gasped. Her thoughts flew away. Because these children were Hansel and Gretel. It would not be fried children as the main course, but roast witch with a big helping of blood.

JOSH WHEELER (11)
Chiltern Hills Academy, Chesham

THE CHASE

Bang! There was a loud sound of a gun. *Bang*! There it was again. There was a cry. 'Run Maleficent run.' She started to run towards the forest into the undergrowth. She was out of breath. She crouched down and lurked in the shadows. She heard a guard call. He screamed and she heard sounds as if he was being dragged through the weeds and leaves... what could it be? Maleficent peeked out from behind a bush and she saw a pair of beady, yellow eyes and it felt as if they were looking into her soul...

EMILIA BOTH D'ANGELO (11)
Chiltern Hills Academy, Chesham

THE GOLDEN APPLE

She was trapped. All she had was the picturesque view from the window. Her name was Rapunzel. She had the longest, most stunning golden hair anyone had seen. One day as she was staring dreamily out the window she saw a boy. He had shiny black hair and his emerald green eyes were twinkling in the distance. He was being chased, 'Please let down your hair!' he yelled. She let it down and he climbed quickly. 'Thank you!' he exclaimed with a relived expression. He handed her a golden apple. She took a bite. Poison trickled down her lips.

NIAMH CONNORS (11)
Chiltern Hills Academy, Chesham

A QUEST FOR A BEAST

It's been three months since Benjamin, son of Beauty and the Beast, left home. However, Benjamin was isolated from the world around him, due to the curse he inherited from his father. Now his quest is to find his true love, someone to lift the villainous curse.

It's felt like eternity, thought Benjamin. As he pondered this, he saw her. At first sight Benjamin knew that she would break his curse. The girl had a river of long hair, black like the night. Benjamin knew of this girl, 'Hello?' a soft voice murmured behind his ear. Their eyes met.

ABIGAIL RACHEL ALHADEFF (11)
Chiltern Hills Academy, Chesham

THE FURRY COAT

A knock at the door. A heart skips a beat. She opened it gingerly. A glimpse of murky, brown fur. A wolf. A hungry wolf, stepped inside. Grandma was preparing dinner for her grandchild, Red.
'Why hello,' Wolf bellowed. 'I see you have dinner.'
'Not for you Wolf!' yelled Grandma.
Suddenly Wolf reached towards Grandma eagerly, licking his chops. *Ping*! A scream, who was it?
Red had walked out from Grandma's cottage into the windy woods, like the trees were whispering to her, wearing a murky, brown, furry coat and a bow and arrow with fresh, ruby red blood.

STELLA JANSSON WILLIAMS (12)
Chiltern Hills Academy, Chesham

FOR THE SAKE OF HER KINGDOM, SHE DOES

She walks down the aisle in her sparkling white dress. Heels clicking in tune to the music and bouquet in hand. On her head, a single rose woven into her delicate hair. For even though she is now Aurora, her true name will always be Briar Rose. You see, the spell requested a kiss from a prince; not someone she loves. 'Princess Aurora, do you take this man to be your lawfully wedded husband?'
She turns to him and resigns herself to a life she was not brought up for; a marriage for the sake of her kingdom. 'I do.'

BADRIYA CABDALLA
Great Baddow High School, Chelmsford

DARK NIGHTS

Last night I was awoken by an owl sitting on the branch outside my window. The dog started barking louder and louder. Slowly, I crept out of bed and tiptoed down the creaky stairs. I nervously approached the front door with a bright torch.

As I opened the door, I saw a white, foggy shadow appear in the dark, breezy fog. I shouted, 'Hello,' but no one answered me, so I shouted again. The white, foggy shadow started to disappear into the distance of darkness. I anxiously shut the door, not knowing what was really there.

STELLA SADDINGTON (15)
Heybridge Alternative Provision School, Heybridge

SPEEDY JOHNSON

One day Speedy Johnson and his crew got a call because there was a family in trouble. They went as soon as possible. They were trapped in a house at the green.

When the crew arrived, there were millions of zombies eating people and trying to get into the house, banging on the windows and doors. One zombie tried to bite Speedy Johnson! One of the crew bit the zombie and turned it into a superhero. So they had an idea to bite all the zombies to turn them into superheroes. They got their families out safely.

LEON JOHNSON (12)
Heybridge Alternative Provision School, Heybridge

John The Zombie Killer

John the zombie killer saw a bright flare above the local park. Rushing in to help, with no regard for his own safety, John fought each and every zombie until there were no more. The villagers didn't know how to repay him so they invited him to stay in the village to help defend their homes. They built fences with barbed wire on top and wooden stakes around the perimeter. No zombie was getting in easily! He stayed with them until he knew they were ready to fight for themselves. After an emotional farewell, John left seeking his next adventure.

Archie Kite (13)
Heybridge Alternative Provision School, Heybridge

THE ZALLIAN PRINCESS

As I entered space, I thought about my mission to Mars. Out of nowhere, a meteor hit the wing of the rocket. I landed on the pink planet, Zallian. Stepping off the rocket, I was surrounded by aliens. They asked me to help them find the Zallian princess. I agreed. Searching the planet, I suddenly heard a scream. It was the princess. Freeing her, she demanded, 'You must marry me.' There were guards surrounding me. I was trapped. Suddenly, I got free. I was running so fast, I felt sick. I got my rocket and launched, waving.

BETHANY THORPE-KEEN (14)
Heybridge Alternative Provision School, Heybridge

UNTITLED

Suzie and John lived in Barbados; a small hot island with palm trees and long sandy beaches. They spent their time scuba diving and hunting for treasure. They swam through a hole in the coral reef and found a hidden world. Merpeople were swimming in a pool set in the ancient ruins of Atlantis. They felt scared but excited and couldn't wait to explore.

The merpeople hid when they saw them. Carefully entering the ruins, they spotted a half-filled treasure chest. As they tried to open it, the merpeople appeared angrily through the doors and windows, and...

ELLIOTT CLARK (12)
Heybridge Alternative Provision School, Heybridge

THE HOUSE OF SWEETS

Slam! With one swift movement the oven door shut. Both children, Hansel and Gretel, were cooking nicely. They would make a delicious meal later. The witch cackled. Trying to shove her in the oven? What were they thinking? At least she had found them before their father. Her bony claws had gripped their shoulders. The children were becoming lovely and crispy now. Their skin was shrivelling. That would make a tasty snack. She dragged the bodies out of the oven, and took them home to her cold stone castle. Why would she live in a house made of sweets? Honestly!

ANNA HUBBARD (13)
High School for Girls, Gloucester

RUN, RUN AS FAST AS YOU CAN

'You can't catch me I'm the gingerbread man,' he scowls. The ravenous children chase him with drooling mouths.
'We're going to eat you,' they giggle.
The gingerbread man turns - fierce revenge building in his eyes. He plots his escape. 'I'll set a trap.' Running ahead, he spots the perfect snare. Hearing the excitable children close by, cunningly he says, 'You can't catch me I'm the gingerbread man!' Laughing sinisterly, he looks down into the hole, his plan has worked. Mouth salivating and stomach rumbling, he slyly looks, points and whispers, 'Now I am going to eat you!'

NEENA PATEL (13)
High School for Girls, Gloucester

SLEEPY'S TASTY!

Snow White was a frequent visitor to the dwarfs' cottage. Otherwise she stayed in her tiny cabin by the river, opposite the forest. Every day she plotted her next move. One day the dwarf, Sleepy, had disappeared. This particular day Snow White never showed up at the dwarfs' house. She wasn't in her cabin either. There was a trail of footprints leading into the thickest part of the forest. They had to find Sleepy. The trail led to a toasty fire, with Snow White eating a large turkey. All Snow said was, 'Sleepy's tasty, which one of you is next?'

JESSICA DUFFY (12)
High School for Girls, Gloucester

THE ELVES

Crash! The elves were cruel and definitely not stealthy. They tiptoed in, needles in hands with only cold burning desire that drove them towards the shoemaker's bed. They worked for hours in the dead of night. For what was to happen was not a pretty sight. They left only two drops of evidence for his wife to see. After all they had come only to scare. Their job was done. The price was paid. The elves escaped with one swift movement through the open front door. 'Argh!' screamed the shoemaker's wife, for the only thing left was his glistening blood.

EMILY THOMSON (12)
High School for Girls, Gloucester

THE KID AND THE EMPEROR

An emperor in the Far East was growing old and knew it was time to choose his successor. Instead of choosing one of his assistants or his children, he decided something different. He called young people in the kingdom together one day. He said, 'It's time for me to step down and choose the next emperor. I have decided to choose one of you.'

The kids were shocked! The emperor continued, 'I'm going to give each of you a seed, a special seed that I want you to plant. Come back in one year with what you have grown.'

FATIMA ISHAAQ
Islington Arts & Media School, London

THE HERO NEXT DOOR

The hero called Max was as strong as the Undertaker, but has a weakness. The weakness is his leg, he's having surgery so that's the time to attack as fast as Mark and as smart as Josh; he got killed with his blade. He was poisoned with his hand when his blade hit. That was the end for the Undertaker. They made a grave that stank. He was discriminated by everyone because he was evil. Max on the other hand was a saviour and was known throughout the world and his mum was proud; he was popular and famous.

ABDIRAHMAN HASHI (12)
Islington Arts & Media School, London

Twisted Story Of Little Red Riding Hood

On a stormy winter's night, when the wind blows with its might she walks alone through the wood. Her name's Little Red Riding Hood. The willow trees along the forest trail away their empty branches and wait.

'I will eat you,' the whisper sounded near, sending Riding Hood into a state of fear. Clutching her basket she spun around. Only to meet darkness from sky to awake and alert. Her thumping heart giving her a torment. To go on or to go back, she couldn't decide. How she wished her mother was by her side.

Nasro Mohamoud (12)
Islington Arts & Media School, London

GOLDILOCKS THE BEAR HUNTER

Goldilocks the bear hunter had a target; she had been chasing them and tracking them; or should I say for a while now. And you may think why it takes so much preparation; well these are not normal bears; they are evil. They have a porridge recipe which is poisonous and has an irresistible smell that will make you eat it without any self-control.

So she went into the bears' cave with her gas mask, specifically for the porridge, but little did she know she was no match for the bears or the porridge. She was not coming back!

ALYON ZEKAJ (14)
Islington Arts & Media School, London

Long Is The Way (Instruments Of Darkness)

She launched herself through the portal. Bruised, bloody, her black fighting gear ripped. She knew where she was. She'd escaped at last. Having a feeling of shallow hope, she sprinted out the door. She ran. Stumbling inside the Institute, she stopped.
There she was - Tatiana - with black blood tears running down her cheeks as she clutched a small, semi-circular garden scythe at her own throat. Tatiana gestured for Sage to look back. She turned to face a mirror. She blinked, her eyes flicking black as her reflection changed. It was her father's. 'Sage, you're still here, in Hell, with me.'

ANDREEA STANESCU (14)
Islington Arts & Media School, London

Uglyrella

Once upon a time there was a teenage girl with the name of Layla. It was the last day on Friday in school; she went to buy some clothes. Twenty minutes later she arrived at Lidl's where they sell the best clothes. She went to the clothes section where a pair of unbranded shoes grabbed her eyes. She took them to the till and gave the £4 and she left Lidl's in joy, as she left a hideous looking boy looked at her and she fell in love, before she got attracted she ran away but she dropped her shoe.

SAIF AHMED (13)
Islington Arts & Media School, London

Little Red Riding Hood

One day a little girl, who was wearing a red cape, was skipping in the forest towards her grandma's house. She was really excited! On her she saw colourful flowers (on the roof), she thought it would be great to give her grandma some flowers, so she decided to pick some. After about ten minutes she continued walking; as she arrived she saw massive footprints! The girl dropped the flowers and ran into the house. As she came close she saw blood on the floor, 'Grandma!' She started panicking. She went inside and saw her grandma dead on the floor.

Basak Uzunsakal (13)
Islington Arts & Media School, London

Awoken And Ugly

Awoken, you see a beast. The cracking mirrors were shattering into pieces, who is this beast? She made the door creak, the noise would cut your ears off. As she opened the door with her slimy hand she could see her face with a hidden mirror.

'You're hideous!' exclaimed an outside voice. The beast turned around only to see another soul that was better than hers. However, in darkness she's a beauty, her face glows like the stars in the sky. In darkness everyone says, 'You're beautiful!' But she can never see her gorgeousness because in darkness she lies asleep.

Sami Bessadi (13)
Islington Arts & Media School, London

THE MAGIC SOUP

There was a mystery girl and a dark knight fighting with a wizard. The girl got cursed and became a frog.

She was very sad. She hopped away and jumped into a bowl of creamy soup. She swam for a while, then jumped out.

Meanwhile, the dark knight was still fighting the wizard. Some people came along and got cursed too, so there were a lot of frogs hopping about!

The dark knight laid a trap to catch the wizard. He threw him some soup! That broke the spell, everyone turned back into themselves and the wizard became a frog.

JOSHUA WHEELER (14)
Lakeside School, Chandlers Ford

MURDERED BY HER CLOSEST FRIEND

The fairest lady skips carefree home, Snow White. But her friends are to betray her because friendship never lasts... 'Do you have it?' Grumpy nods vigorously, brandishing the object. This is hastily snatched away; placed on the bed. The seven dwarfs hear footsteps, and crouch behind the curtains with baited breath... Snow White places the apple to her lips, biting deep into the juicy skin... falling lightly to the floor. Merrily, those evil dwarfs hack at her, blunt axes inflicting much pain on their victim. Her eyes open - she awakes. They leave her, to die an agonising, prolonged death...

ELLIE HARWOOD (12)
Malmesbury School, Malmesbury

I THOUGHT WE WERE FRIENDS

I was helpless. The brutal flame devoured the seated planks. It was weeks later, we had barely been surviving. We helped people whose lives were affected by the fire. We found a cave. 'Food!' A bear strode up to us, he was going to attack me, but Gran stepped in and stabbed it. 'Thanks.' There was no reply, she was staring at me and coming closer until I was in a corner. She said, 'It's all over,' as she sank her teeth into my neck, ripping out my spine. I lay lifeless on the floor, her feasting on my flesh.

TOM WALDRON (13)
Malmesbury School, Malmesbury

Francesca's Dream

There was once an inquisitive girl called Francesca. She had an extravagant lifestyle and made elaborate choices which reflected on her wild personality. One day, Francesca found herself mysteriously deep inside a cave with only a speck of light penetrating the darkness. This was just enough light for her to notice the dark figure feasting and devouring an innocent corpse. This emotionless monster shocked her and sent shivers down her delicate spine. As this monster turned and stared at her, she realised this thing had the face of a bewildered, newborn baby. It began to approach... Francesca woke up.

Jack Cloke (13)
Malmesbury School, Malmesbury

KING MARCUS

Anne screamed. Gone. Marcus was King of Browan and he was missing. After alerting the people of Browan, a strange little man came to her. 'My name,' he sang, 'is Pied Piper. I can solve worries, I can find Marcus for £999.' Anne decided to try. She paid the piper; he skipped away, supposedly to find Marcus. 100 miles away was a crooked house, the piper's. In there, tied up, was Marcus, 'I got my money, but a king I will not give.' The piper cackled, 'before I move on a king pie I shall eat. Goodbye King Marcus.'

HANNAH BROWN (12)
Malmesbury School, Malmesbury

TEN YEARS

He was running away from something which couldn't be avoided.
He had been chosen. It was entertaining for them to torment him.
Thump, every night it would come. It made the boy angry, with his
anger he grew stronger. He told himself he wouldn't be defeated.
He built a staff in the hope that it would send them away. This only
provoked the ghost. It used the staff to send him to Hell... 'Do you
like it?'
'Yeah, seems like a good screenplay.'
'It's just a start, took me ten years in hell to write.'

OLIVER KLINKENBERG
Malmesbury School, Malmesbury

UNTITLED

One day there was a family walking in a churchyard, when they heard a noise coming from one of the graves. They were very, very scared. They did not move for a while until they saw a light. 'Run,' said Dad but the little boy stood there. The rest of them ran to the light. When they got there, it was an old church.

One of them said, 'Where is Jeff?' They went back for him but he was not there.

'He has been killed,' said Mum. She started crying. The old man was sad...

TOBY RYMAN (13)
Malmesbury School, Malmesbury

THE FIGHT FOR THE SAVANNAH

It was a sunny day at the savannah. All you could hear was the scream of the evil King Cobra. The animals had enough of the evil king's rule. Ernie was a kind elephant. He wanted what was best for the savannah. So one dark night Ernie and the animals set out to kill him. It was dark and cold. They crept to the door; Ernie followed by the gang. The dagger was sharp, about to stab. Ernie felt something; the king had bitten him. He painfully fell.
Later that day he died. Cobra made the savannah a living hell.

TOM POULTON (12)
Malmesbury School, Malmesbury

THE THREE BEARS' REVENGE

One day the three bears decided that revenge was in order for Goldilocks because of what she did to them. So the daddy, mummy and baby bear set off into the woods to Goldilocks' house. Once they reached her house, Daddy pushed open the unlocked door. Baby ran through and sat on all the chairs ripping them up after. Mummy ate her porridge left on the work top and Daddy jumped on the bed. Then Goldilocks rushed in to find Mummy, Daddy and Baby asleep on her bed. She turned off the lights and went to clean up the mess.

BETH PIKE (12)
Malmesbury School, Malmesbury

GEORGE AND THE DRAGON

Once upon a time in a mighty kingdom, there lived King Richard and Prince George. One day King Richard ordered George to kill the big green dragon. George set out to kill the dragon. A while later he found the forest, home to the dragon. He walked in and saw the dragon. He raised up his sword to strike the big green dragon, but then it spoke. 'All I want is a friend.' So George took the dragon back to the kingdom and they became the best of friends, just what the dragon wanted, and they lived happily ever after.

WILLIAM COLLETT (13)
Malmesbury School, Malmesbury

Ghost Child

A horrible stepbrother takes his sister to a haunted forest. She is pushed through a hole in the ground. When she tumbles to the bottom it opens to a small room. Her heart starts to beat, she can hear giggles and crying. Little did she know that this place was haunted. She feels something crawl up her back, she thought it was a spider, but really a ghost child's hand. She started to turn around to see red glowing eyes. She started to scream, but no one could hear her. Then the eyes got closer and closer and closer.

Jolene Elizabeth Way (13)
Malmesbury School, Malmesbury

A Giant Meal

'How dare he? He thinks he can come in here and steal my precious eggs? Well think again. My wife may be understanding but I am not. This is an outrage. I will travel to the end of the Earth to get back what was stolen from me. I must begin my journey into the unknown.' Below the clouds, I see a tiny figure climbing down. I start to descend, gaining on Jack. We finally meet at the bottom of the stalk, and let's just say no one saw the boy after that; no one but my stomach.

Jasmine Barron (13)
Malmesbury School, Malmesbury

RETURNING THE FAVOUR

Baby Bear's hungry, but we're too far from home. So, a dark, windy path is the one to follow. Then, a cottage covered in poison ivy; sweet singing tunes coming from inside. Soon after, silence. We creep up to the cottage and knock. No answer. I push open the unlocked door, and gesture for the other two bears to follow. My gaze follows the steam trail to a pie sitting on a cooling rack, mockingly. But then... a swish of gold, and my gaze quickly averts. A golden-haired girl narrows her eyes... We were tricked into thinking she'd gone.

IMOGEN WALL
Malmesbury School, Malmesbury

LITTLE RED RIDING HOOD AND THE THREE BEARS

Little Red Riding Hood was strolling through the woods on a sunny morning. As she got to the end of the woods there were three bears looking rather puzzled. Little Red Riding Hood took the three bears home for lunch. Her grandmother was just making her lunch. She didn't want the three bears in her house but Little Red Riding Hood said they were really nice bears. But her grandmother did not agree. Little Red Riding Hood tells them lunch is ready. Unfortunately, the three bears were terribly ill because her grandmother put a horrible poison in all their food.

ELLA WOOLLIAMS (13)
Malmesbury School, Malmesbury

Goldilocks And The Three Bears

Once there lived a young girl who had golden hair; Goldilocks was her name. She loved to venture through the misty woods. One day she stumbled across a house, a house like no other; it held inside three beds, a large one, a medium sized one, and a little one. Goldilocks wandered into a kitchen, there before her held three bowls of porridge. She tried each one, the first was too hot; the second too cold, but the last was just right. Just as she finished the last bowl, three bears stormed in and ate her in one whole bite.

Jacob Humphries (14)
Malmesbury School, Malmesbury

SAFE HAVEN

My family, my neighbours, everyone gone. We thought we were safe. We were wrong. Our town claimed to be the safest place on Earth. They took us in, protected us but now the safe haven has fallen. They ran at us, attacked the people around me, everywhere we ran they were there to stop us. We ran out of options, my children ran away from them. I only hope they are still alive. Some call them walkers, some biters, we call them death. But where do you go when the safe haven falls?

LOUIS RADFORD (13)
Malmesbury School, Malmesbury

THE MIXED TITLE

A mind-boggling red cloak stirred the prey's eyes. Small and vicious. One may not pass. Sinister eyes glow and taunt its prey. Three bears and a gingerbread man pass by collecting oat and ginger, but sin yet to drown them. A splash of red caught in the corner of their eye. A tenderly crunch of leaves. The bears and the gingerbread man become wary for what may pounce upon them. Sticky porridge flew out the trees acting as a web barrier and trapped them. Fear whistled around them for what may be around. Out walked Grandma.

MAX HILL-PALMER (14)
Malmesbury School, Malmesbury

THE GOLDEN PORRIDGE!

Goldilocks, after being chased, then went back to the little cottage in the woods, following the smell of the three bears' porridge... Slowly, she walked in the wooden door, sneakily one by one she looked in each room, finally the kitchen... the coast was clear, she ran silently into the white room. Suddenly, out of nowhere, Baby Bear appeared and Goldilocks ran, Mummy and Daddy Bear grabbed her and dragged her into the kitchen and chucked her into boiling water on the stove and turned her into golden porridge. They invited their friends, the witch and the wolf to enjoy.

MOLLI BLAKE (13)
Malmesbury School, Malmesbury

THE CREATURE

A dark, gloomy night and the moon shone brightly. A creature, fierce, heart-stopping - everyone's nightmare. This was no ordinary pig! One night, at the stroke of 12 in the nearby fields, flashes of movement were reported by villagers, cows dead, still as statues. People starving as if slaves, prisoners in their own homes; no matter how hard they worked no money left to eat. This creature destroyed everything, brushing through villages as quiet as a mouse, as stealthy as a viper, killing everything in its way until nothing was left; no one was safe.

LUKE ROGERS (13)
Malmesbury School, Malmesbury

SNOWMAN

I've never liked snowmen. It's the way they look at you - gives me the creeps. Brrrrr! I'll tell you a story about the time I came face to face with one. Here goes...

It was when I was three and I was out playing with my older sister. We made a really scary snowman. But what I did not know was - it came alive! It rampaged my street and ate everyone's candy, ruining everyone's day.

Then one day, the sun came out and everything was fine. The abominable snowman had fled... but the fairies had not!

LEONIE PALMER (12)
Putteridge High School, Luton

DEAD LITTLE RED RIDING HOOD

I was strolling through the wood, when something jumped out, a
wolf in fact. He stood there licking his lips. I ran screaming all the
way till I got to my nan's. The woodcutter was there, he told me
to get in the cupboard. So I did, slamming the door behind me. I
heard something, it was the wolf, so I opened the door to see the
woodcutter and my nan lying there. I picked up the axe and ran at
the wolf. We both fell to the ground screaming till I realised, I got him.
The wolf was dead!

OCEA COHEN (14)
Redruth School, Redruth

His Last Wish

Have you ever wondered what someone's last wish is? One night, in a forest unknown there was a lone man. After every couple of footsteps, he'd look behind to check there was no one behind him. On one of his checks he noticed a wolf behind him. Suddenly it started to charge at him, so he thought he wouldn't be able to run away, so he made his last wish. The wolf ran at him and pounced on him, and then ran off and the dead body had one huge scratch mark on its chest with a deep wound beside.

TYLER SELLARS (12)
Saltash.net Community School, Saltash

THE EX-KILLER

There were eighteen. Eighteen children killed at once. How? How could someone do that? People call her, it or him the 'ex-killer'. No one knows their full identity, apart from that they're tall and slender.
'How many attacks have there been?' asked Jo (CSI agent).
'The last attack would make 43,' replied Daniel (scientist).
They were in the DC National Laboratory observing the last terrorist attack. So far they had probably got through 10% of the evidence. As you could probably tell this was a big attack, that means a big investigation. Will Jo and Daniel solve the attack?

BEN SUMMERFIELD (12)
Saltash.net Community School, Saltash

Frozen

Elsa and Anna were the two beautiful princesses of Ardendelle. But Elsa had cryokinetic powers. Elsa and Anna had a big fight. Through emotion, Elsa struck at Anna's heart with her powers. Anna died... Through grief of Anna's death, Elsa went crazy. She turned the whole of Ardendelle into a deep winter. She found Olaf and put a curse on him to never be happy again. She built herself an ice palace and lay on the frozen floor. She hasn't woken up since, but that may not be the case for long...

Lowenna Savery (11)
Saltash.net Community School, Saltash

Untitled

Mr Bunny was prancing along happily in Bunny Land. Suddenly, his friend Mr Magicat Floating Goldfish came up to him and said, 'Can you help me please? Mr Nibbling has gone missing again!' They soon found Mr Nibbling. Then the floor opened up, they descended into the darkness and died.

JACK SIMMONDS (11)
Saltash.net Community School, Saltash

FAULTY PARTS

There once was a man named Bob, he loved flying. One day it went wrong - there was a jolt coming from the front. What was it though? Then the instruments failed, Bob was surprised to say the least. What he was in, had a good reliability record. What caused it, was beyond him. Suddenly the now slightly petrified man from Swansea heard this brushing sound, which turned out to be from the trees - this was reality, not a nightmare. More sounds were coming from somewhere unknown, *crash!* All was silent, then a cloud of smoke suddenly rose.

WILLIAM MIRAKIAN (12)
Saltash.net Community School, Saltash

AM I DEAD?

The gravel slipped beneath her feet and left her no choice but to fall to the ground. Slowly, she picked herself up. She had just fled from the palace, looking like a mess. She then ran to the forest. Now she was lost. Suddenly, a figure appeared in the darkness. It wore a long, ripped cloak and you could just see yellow glowing eyes, even with its hood. It ran. She picked up courage and said, 'Who are you?' It didn't answer. All her fear was now slowly coming back, so she ran, but she couldn't. She was already dead.

OLIVIA KESSELL (12)
Saltash.net Community School, Saltash

HANSEL AND GRETEL

Fairy tales aren't all, 'happily ever after'. The truth is much worse. This is the story of Hansel and Gretel...

Once upon a time there were two children. Their names were Hansel and Gretel. They stumbled upon a house, a candy house. They hammered at the door screaming for help. The door creaked open... Cautiously they stepped inside. The door slammed behind him and the darkness swallowed them whole. An oven began to glow, lighting the room to show blood and chewed flesh scattered on the floor. The smell of their burning skin drifted through the forest...

ARCHIE FLEMING (12)
Saltash.net Community School, Saltash

Witch Slayers

The clock struck midnight, all the children were locked away. Houses were boarded up. Suddenly the witch cackled, an ear-piercing scream struck fear into the hearts of everyone. After surviving a witch as children, Hansel and Gretel had been hunting witches and taking their revenge. Hansel ran for the witch, sword in hand. The witch cast a spell. *Bang!* Hansel was dead, Gretel screamed with grief. She ran for the witch who was stood by the cliff. Gretel pushed the witch but the witch grabbed Gretel's leg and they fall into a long painful death.

Jago Christopher Adams (12)
Saltash.net Community School, Saltash

CHOP, CHOP, CHOP

Jerold the unicorn was galloping in Cherryland when he heard a rustling noise in the raspberry bush. So he galloped up to the bush and peered over. Suddenly, Jerold jumped up, falling onto a bed of cherries. *Squish!* He was covered in juice, it looked like he'd been in a horror film. Jerold stood up and ran for his life, a shadow was lurking behind him, ready to pounce. All of a sudden a large dark figure appeared in front of Jerold, he screamed for help, but it was too late. A knife appeared and then *chop, chop, chop, chop...*

CARISSA AMBROSE (12)
Saltash.net Community School, Saltash

112

UNTITLED

After the little mermaid saved the prince from a shipwreck, he decided to try and find her. The prince searched and searched, no luck! He even got his servants to search.

The little mermaid decided to tell the prince. After she told the prince, he took the little mermaid to the castle's kitchen. He said to the chef, 'I want sushi.' Unfortunately, the mermaid was cooked and the prince ate her up.

DARCY DYMOND (12)
Saltash.net Community School, Saltash

THE SLAP

The three bears went for a walk to the park and left their house door open. Meanwhile, Goldilocks felt tired and walked into the house. She strolled upstairs and went to sleep in their bed. Dad Bear felt tired and walked into the house, not realising Goldilocks was in his bed. So he went to sleep.

Mum and Child Bear walked back to the house to find Dad Bear in the same bed as Goldilocks. When Dad Bear woke up, Mum Bear gave him a big slap and they got divorced.

OWEN FISHER (11)
Saltash.net Community School, Saltash

Grim Tale

There were two kids who lived near the woods. One day they went out and played and took a few things with them; bread, water, etc in a bag. But this idea didn't end well because the children got lost and couldn't find their way home. But they didn't care because they found a house made of chocolate. The kids loved chocolate, but instead of going to the house they just walked away from it, not knowing what to do. They managed to find their way home but realised no one was there because they had been eaten by monsters.

Josh Griffiths (12)
Saltash.net Community School, Saltash

THE DISAPPEARING HOOD

The wolf ran towards the ever-nearing red-hooded girl. It was within biting distance. And then, it wasn't there. Gone. It was now as far away as it was when he started running. He was confused. He started running again but the same thing happened. He decided to run the opposite way and he saw it right in front of him. He bit it but there was no girl there, just another wolf, almost exactly the same as him. He turned around and the hood was back. He turned around and hit the wolf. All went black.

FINLEY GILCHRIST (12)
Saltash.net Community School, Saltash

THE WOODEN MAN

A little orphan boy, who longed for his own father, collected wood, found some nails, borrowed tools and created his 'perfect' dad by following every detail as instructed. No feature was overlooked. The boy was proud of his achievement, the result was perfect. The boy wanted to be like his strong and handsome dad who would read to him, teach him, play with him and make the boy feel safe. But the boy realised there was only wood and nails holding his dad together. So he could never make a father who would love him from the heart.

LOTTIE RYDER-WEARNE (12)
Saltash.net Community School, Saltash

RED

One day there was a pretty girl who lived with her horrible mother, who one day sent Red to her granny's but Red didn't like her gran so she decided to eat half of the snacks her mum had packed her to give to her gran.
She forgot the way so she used Google, when she was almost there she saw a sign. When she got to Gran's her gran was listening to Uptown Funk which was a surprise. When she said hello her gran threw a hissy fit so a nice wolf saved her from her grandma.

ALYSHA BAKER (12)
Saltash.net Community School, Saltash

PRINCE CHARLES AND THE TOWER

Once upon a time, there was a prince called Charles. He came across a tower where a beautiful, long-haired, blonde girl was sitting on the window sill singing to herself. He asked to climb up the tower by her hair, but when he did, he fell like a sack of spuds. They were hair extensions and she screamed, taking off her mask to reveal a green-faced, ugly witch. Charles ran and ran into the woods as fast as he could to escape the horror he'd just witnessed. He never returned to the tower.

LUCY JAYNE ADDIS (15)
Saltash.net Community School, Saltash

THE TWISTED TALE OF THE PIED PIPER

The Pied Piper is known for bad deeds, in this story it's a little different. The animals bore the brunt of them. On a stormy night, the Pied Piper was polishing his flutes. The animals had a chance of kidnapping him, so Badger dug under the small cottage and broke the gas pipe. He struck a match. *Boom!* The Pied Piper was a little out of it, but okay. The animals dragged him to Rabbit's house, who had a recording of the flutes. The Pied Piper listened to it for 365 days. After this, he promised to destroy the flutes.

KIEREN KEITH (11)
Saltash.net Community School, Saltash

29/02/10

One day, Jim's life was turned upside down. It all started on the 29th February 2010. Jim was out on his leap year walk with a couple of his mates. He was talking to his friends about their favourite cars when one by one, his friends disappeared. Jim was still talking about his favourite car, even when there was no one left to listen. The moment Jim turned around, horror struck him. His friends had gone. Propelled by fear, Jim ran further into the woods until a silent figure dropped out of a tree and assassinated him.

MATTHEW THOMAS (12)
Saltash.net Community School, Saltash

THE STORY OF CINDERELLA

Ever since Cinders, otherwise known as Cinderella, was born she loved to dance and dress up.

At the age of nine, after her father died she was sent by her mother, who was very ill, to go and live with her auntie and three wealthy daughters, they all disliked Cinders and thought she was ugly and disgusting.

When the night of the prince's ball came they forced Cinders to do all the work and to make them show a little beauty. As they were about to leave, Cinders jumped ahead into their carriage and sped off, they were left raging!

PHOEBE TURNER (12)
Saltash.net Community School, Saltash

CINDERELLA'S DODGY EXPERIENCE

Once upon a time, on the second ball, Cinderella didn't feel like dancing, so she left. But from out of nowhere, the prince appeared holding two tablets. He forced them down her throat. Suddenly, her eyes dilated and she felt as if she could dance all night. She partied all night, drinking only water by the gallon because of her never-ending thirst. After the party, she locked herself in the bathroom and choked on the water she had been drinking all night. Moral of the story is, carry a rape alarm and don't do drugs, because they are bad.

WILLIAM CASABAYO (14)
Saltash.net Community School, Saltash

Peter And Tinkerbell's Adventure

Once upon a time, there was a boy, dressed in emerald green silk, called Peter Pan. His best friend was a flirtatious fairy called Tinkerbell. They had wonderful adventures together. But, in the world of Neverland, there was a horrible pirate that went by the name of Captain Hook. He was a wacky man, always trying to steal treasure from innocent people. One delightful sunset, Peter saw Captain Hook stealing some treasure from an innocent young pirate. Peter got ready by chucking fairy dust over himself. He jumped out the window. It turns out it was salt. Peter died.

Joshua Middleton (14)
Saltash.net Community School, Saltash

THE ENCHANTED FOREST

The forest is full of chirping birds and the sky is full of fireflies, giving the forest an enchanting look. Little Red Riding Hood is searching the enchanted forest to find ingredients for her grandma. Suddenly, the wicked fairy of the forest appears. The wicked fairy giggles and begins chanting strange words whilst wiggling her wrinkled fingers in Red Riding Hood's direction. Red Riding Hood realises that she is casting a spell and grabs her mirror to deflect the spell. A green light is launched at Riding Hood, but is deflected and turns the wicked fairy into an ugly pigeon!

HARLEY RUSSELL (14)
Saltash.net Community School, Saltash

LITTLE MER TWIST

Little Mermaid was sick of not being able to go up to the land which she always dreamed of. Her father did not allow her. One day she went against her father's wishes and went up to the surface. He forbade her to ever go back again. Going up to the surface to find her lover lying on the rock bleeding out from the heart. Crying her eyes out, she decided she couldn't live without him, so she killed herself as she could not live without her lover anymore. Both lying on the rock. Love together, death together.

AMY DRUMMOND (14)
Saltash.net Community School, Saltash

THE TRUTH BEHIND JIMMY CHOO

The clock struck 12. 'I have to go,' she squealed, waving her golden locks behind her as she began to run to the door. The prince, confused, followed Cinderella quickly so she could not escape without him. One glass slipper remained and to his surprise it was clearly one of a kind! Prince Charming picked up the sparkling shoe and studied its features in detail. An idea struck his mind and 'Jimmy Choo' was born! The prince declined his offer to become a king, so he could become a billionaire with his new line of shoes, living happily ever after.

DAISY BUDD (15)
Saltash.net Community School, Saltash

Bye Bye Rapunzel

There was a woman called Rapunzel and she was placed in a tower after she was rescued from a castle by a fairy. One day, a man came to the bottom of the tower and said, 'Hello.'
Rapunzel poked her head out the window and let down her golden hair. She said, 'Climb up!'
So he started to climb, but he suddenly hit the ground with a *bang*! Rapunzel's hair followed after him. The ground was red with blood from where Rapunzel had fallen out the tower and cracked her head open with her brain next to her.

JOHN PHARE (14)
Saltash.net Community School, Saltash

THE CASTING PIGEON

A little girl called Red Riding Hood decided to walk into the forest, but she was followed by a wicked fairy who decided to turn her into a pigeon. The fairy then put her in a cage but Little Red Riding Hood could still talk. Goldilocks rushed there to find Little Red Riding Hood as a pigeon. The wicked fairy tried to put the spell on Goldilocks but Little Red Riding Hood grabbed Goldilocks' mirror and reflected the spell back to the fairy. She became an ugly pigeon.

RHYS BRADLEY (15)
Saltash.net Community School, Saltash

MURDERER INSIDE

I stand in a deserted church but I don't feel like the only soul present. I hear footsteps echoing in the hall. Something catches my eye. Rapid flashes. I sprint towards the door but it slams shut! 'I've been expecting you...' utters a raspy voice. I gaze around but there's no one to be seen. 'Right behind you, darling,' it croaks. I grab a piece of broken wood and pound it with all my strength. Little did I know, I just murdered my husband. Oh no. It felt incredible! Suddenly, I feel the urge to kill..

NATASHA PENIC (14)
The Business Academy Bexley, Erith

INSANITY

It'd been a month. A month of unease as the feeling of being watched took over the girl. Once able to enjoy life outside of home; she'd visit the park blissfully until the fateful day she caught a glance of it, lasting a single second. Now, it was in her prison of a house, she was sure. Finally, the night came as she woke to the decrepit shell of a woman at the end of her bed. 'It's time,' she uttered and finally it all made sense. The girl, looking in a mirror took her life with no fear.

LAURA THACKRAY (14)
The Business Academy Bexley, Erith

TURN OF EVENTS OF SNOW WHITE

The prince crusaded bravely through the sparkling azure of the vegetated forest. It was ancient albeit dense and majestic. Light filtered through, illuminating it and making it simply ethereal. Suddenly, something that shimmered intensely captured his eye. He plodded steadily toward the blinding light, intent in unearthing the celestial source. A spell-blinding casket made of glass. Inside, was an unworldly human. Skin as white as snow, lips as red as roses. He crept forward. Suddenly, she rose and wrapped her hands around him. Slowly, the life drained out of him. His pulse dropped and she was finally happy.

DULCE LOPES (14)
The Business Academy Bexley, Erith

Unfortunate Turn Of Events

Her heart thumped loudly as she heard the deep footsteps, followed by a low and rapid growl. This was it, she knew she was done for. The door opened, slowly creaking with every push. Three tall brown figures approached her under the bed, but as they came closer, she recognised them, the bears, her old foe. With that sudden realisation, Goldilocks jumped out from underneath her bed and *slash!* Off with their heads! And after all the drama had ended, Goldilocks skipped home carrying with her three coats of fur and meat that could last her all year.

Omorinola Mark (14)
The Business Academy Bexley, Erith

LIKE FATHER, LIKE SON

As Oliver crept closer, he heard a bang! The arsenic infused bullet pierced his dark, dry skin and out came thick, crimson blood. The loud cry of a woman came, 'You now have three hours to live.' The metallic taste of blood filled his mouth as he ran after her. They got closer to a worn down shack and as he entered she disappeared. The stench of a rotten, mangled corpse filled his nose and mouth and his eyes began to water. The dark black cloth that covered the corpse was removed from its head... It was his father.

DANIEL BANIGO (14)
The Business Academy Bexley, Erith

LITTLE RED ROBIN HOOD

My crimson cloak flew behind me, along with my dark, silky hair. Rain sealed my clothes firmly to my skin. I ran further, into the misty forest, when I saw the deceitful creature that ate Nan. As we exchanged eye contact, I realised now was my time to strike. I slowly approached the wolf, gripping my armed bow. With the blink of an eye, the beast, along with my arrows, were gone. Before I had the chance to turn, the sharp head of my arrow pierced through my neck. With blood oozing out, I knew this was the end.

JAKE AYLIFFE (14)
The Business Academy Bexley, Erith

Goldilocks And The Three Bears II (The Poisonous Cottage Pie!

I moped around the woods for hours, in search of food, even a shrivel of mouldy cheese would suffice right now. The air around me suddenly filled with a mouth-watering aroma of freshly cooked cottage pie. My favourite! I darted towards this tempting smell, my golden locks following. I came to my destination, a small cottage. To my delight the door was left wide open with three divine plates calling my name. I voraciously attacked all three. A sharp pain shot through me, I sprinted to the bedroom and here the three vicious bears stabbed me to death.

Ola Hassan (14)
The Business Academy Bexley, Erith

SNOW WITCH AND THE DEADLY APPLE!

The lush apple lay upon the plump velvet cushion. Temptation is hard to resist, despite my knowledge of its wrong doings. I gape at it in awe. The seven friends entice me to take a bite if I dare. I know the capability, as well as its sweet, juicy exterior, it owns a sour consequence. The waiting proved too challenging, my perfectly white teeth tore the surface of the apple and the clear juice cascaded down my chin. Rushing to the mirror, I take a glance at my contorting self. Within minutes I was staring back at a witch!

BHAVINI JETHWA (14)
The Business Academy Bexley, Erith

DANGEROUS DUMPTY

Humpty set off on his menacing journey up Wall Everest. Rocks crumbling, crashing and falling from multiple directions. The higher Humpty gets, the more complicated his mission becomes. Humpty Dumpty's life could end in a matter of seconds! All of a sudden a colossal rock lunges towards him, knocking him off his feet. Humpty Dumpty tries to regain balance, but it's no use, his hands lose grip. His life flashes before his eyes, then Humpty loses consciousness. Splattered across the floor, all the king's horses and all the king's men try to stick him back together again...

ALYSHA TRAVIS (14)
The Business Academy Bexley, Erith

THE CLEVER PREY

The wolf ran, ran as fast as he possibly could. He wouldn't let his dinner go. He finally got to a hut made out of sticks. He ran into it, knocking the hut down. His prey, inches from his sharp white claws, ran to another hut. This time, it was made out of brick. He ran into it, breaking his bones. The prey leaves the brick hut and kills the helpless wolf. Turns out the wolf was not as strong as he thought.

JACK BERNARD STEPHEN BASHFORD (14)
The Business Academy Bexley, Erith

Rapunzel (The True Story)

The year was 1992, a beautiful young girl was born. Everyone was happy, apart from her father. He wasn't happy because he wanted a strong boy so he sent her to an old abandoned castle to learn how to be manly. When she was eighteen her dad went to visit her at the castle. When he arrived at the castle, he had a horrible realisation… she has disappeared. He thought to himself, *how's that possible?* He looked out of the window of the tower… Little did he know Rapunzel hid behind the bed and pushed him out of the window!

Nikolas Bogdanovic (13)
The Business Academy Bexley, Erith

MODERN DAY CINDERELLA

Sadly Mother passed today, now my stepfather will be the man of the house. Life has suddenly become a living hell.

This afternoon we received an invite for Princess Bella's 21st birthday. The most beautiful girl I have ever seen. Hopefully tonight I will catch her eye and ask for her hand in marriage.

The evening of the party came and my stepfather came to the kitchen and delivered the worst news of my life. That I had missed the ball and the girl of my dreams was my new stepmother.

AMITY CARR (14)
Trinity School, Teignmouth

SNOW WHITE RE-WRITTEN

Snow White looked in the mirror. Today, she decided she would be the ugliest of them all. She heard her beautiful stepmother coming and without another thought, she ran out and killed her. Now she decided, was a good time to visit the seven dwarfs. When she arrived at their house she head them talking.
'I don't trust Snow White.'
'Aye, aye!' Filled with anger, she ran in. She saw a gun and without hesitating, they were gone.
Lastly she tortured the handsome prince by a poisoned apple. Never trust a princess, she often isn't human.

EMMA GITTOES (13)
Trinity School, Teignmouth

THROUGH THE NIGHT!

The woman follows the black haired man through the darkness!
They go through the city. Like a ghost the woman keeps on following
him. Suddenly, the man looks behind but sees nothing so keeps
walking. The man is scared and anxious but doesn't look behind.
She follows him silently through the dark night. As the man reaches
his house in the quiet street, the woman still follows him but the man
doesn't know. The man enters his bathroom and looks into the mirror.
He sees nothing, but then... He sees an animal! An animal he saw
before... A vampire!

VIHIRTHAN KANDIAH (13)
Wilson's School, Wallington

143

Still Alive

My eyelids flutter open, and I notice I'm in a dark, confined space, lying down. I hear murmuring, but I feel distant from it, as if I were listening from under the floor. I hear something else; melancholic notes, played by an invisible organ, as if it were a sad occasion. But something is wrong. There is crying. People speak of me like I'm not there, and I realise; I am present at my own funeral. I struggle against the walls of my oak prison, but the thump of piling earth begins. *'Don't bury me,'* I wail. *'I'm still alive...'*

Spyros Stylianopoulos (14)
Wilson's School, Wallington

ARTHUR AND EXCALIBUR

In Cornwall, there was a sword. Excalibur. Arthur removed it. People looked astonished. 'You're our new king,' they shrieked. He was ecstatic. He couldn't wait to get to the job. Ten days later, however, he feels different. He can't handle it. The job of a king is hard. He's scared, he can't handle it. He's confused, he can't handle it. He looks at the sword, it stares back at him, its dark forces take over him. He takes the sword and he can't handle it. He sticks it in his heart and blood pours out. He could not handle it.

DANISH MALIK (14)
Wilson's School, Wallington

HE LIVES AT MURDER

A shadow flickers, he creeps up, searching for yet another victim. It's a town party. Everyone is there. He lurks in the darkness. He takes aim... but then suddenly a hand grips him, a shot is fired from his pistol, scarcely missing the head of this man. The town's people flock in, rage in their eyes. They'd finally found him. The man who's brought terror to this poor town. Murders happening at free will, a shot fired, silence, followed by cheers. Intestines and guts ripped out of his body, stranded on the floor. The letter, an address, the dead living.

SAM BELGROVE (13)
Wilson's School, Wallington